This Little Tiger book
belongs to:

For William, Robin and Tom
~ H W

For Jess, love Aunty Bek xx
~ R H

LITTLE TIGER PRESS
1 The Coda Centre, 189 Munster Road, London SW6 6AW
www.littletiger.co.uk

First published in Great Britain 2014
This edition published 2014

A CIP catalogue record for this book is available from the British Library

Printed in China • LTP/1400/0890/0514

2 4 6 8 10 9 7 5 3 1

Little Puppy
LOST

Holly Webb   Rebecca Harry

LITTLE TIGER PRESS
London

Harry's tail wagged as he raced through the park.
His eyes sparkled, and his ears flapped from side to side
as he looked at all the exciting things.

"Today's our first ever walk, Harry!" Evie said,
giving him a little hug. "Isn't it fun?"

Harry wriggled with happiness. The park was the
most wonderful place he had ever seen!

Suddenly, a bright red ball whisked past Harry's nose. His ears twitched as he flung himself after it. He was so excited, he didn't notice his brand new collar slipping off!

"Come back!" Evie cried, waving his lead. But Harry didn't hear her.

He pounced on the ball with a happy little growl. But then someone else growled – much louder.

Staring down at Harry were two huge dogs.
Harry wriggled backwards. "You can chase my ball,"
he said, in a wobbly whisper.

"Oh no," the biggest dog barked. "We're going
to chase you!"

Harry yelped and raced for the wood.
But the other dogs came
pounding after him,
closer and closer . . .

Through the trees Harry spotted a hole.

He wriggled inside just as the dogs raced by.

He waited, and waited, and waited, then at last

he poked his nose out.

"It's all right. They've gone," a voice said from high above.

Harry squeaked in surprise! Looking down at him was a thin, gingery cat.

"You're too little to be out here on your own," the cat said.

"I'm lost," Harry sniffed. "And I don't know where my best friend Evie is."

"I was lost once too," the cat smiled gently. "Don't worry, I can show you out of this wood."

"Oh, thank you!" the little puppy beamed. "I'm Harry."

"And I'm Ginger!" said the cat. "Follow me!"

Harry trotted after
Ginger. Suddenly a
huge bird flapped out
of the shadows in front
of them.

"Watch out!" Ginger
cried, as Harry
tumbled into a pile
of leaves.

"Do you mind?" snapped a grumpy-looking hedgehog.

"Come on," Ginger sighed. "Almost there."

Harry's ears pricked up happily. Evie would be so pleased to see him!

"Evie! Evie!" Harry barked. But the park
was empty now, dark and silent.

"She's gone," Harry cried as he sank down
on the cold grass. "I want to go home,"
he whimpered.

Ginger gave him a gentle nudge. "We'll find the way –
and we'll find you something to eat, too," he added,
as they set off towards the town.

"Down here?" Harry sniffed uncertainly.

The alley was dark, but something in the bins smelled delicious.

Then he heard a snarl . . .

There in the darkness was a huge white cat.
She hissed at Ginger and slashed at him with
her claws.

Harry growled. There was no time to lose!
He took a deep breath, and . . .

... BARKED and BARKED and BARKED!
The noise echoed round the alley.

The white cat squealed and
shot away in fright.

Ginger stared in amazement.
"Harry!" he cheered. "You're
a hero!"

Harry wagged his tail
shyly, and sniffed around for
something else to eat. But
then he stopped and his nose
quivered. "Oh!" he squeaked.

"What is it?" Ginger asked.

"I can smell home!" Harry
cried as he darted out of the alley.
"It's this way!"

The two friends ran past the brightly-lit
shops and houses until . . .

"This is my house!" Harry cried,
scrabbling at the front door.

"Harry!" Evie raced to scoop him up.
"You came home," she murmured,
   rubbing her cheek against his soft ears.
"We were so worried about you!"

But Harry jumped down.
He'd forgotten Ginger!
"Don't go!" he yelped.
Ginger was trailing out of
the garden, his ears flattened
and sad.
"Have you brought a friend?"
Evie whispered as Harry led
Ginger back up the path.

Evie took them inside and gave
them lots to eat. Then Harry
snuggled up on her knee.

"There's room for you too,"
Evie whispered to Ginger.

The old cat purred happily.
He curled himself around his
friend, and together they fell
fast asleep.

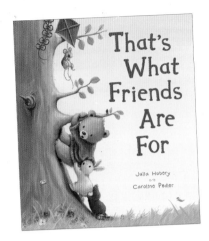

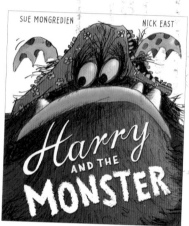

More wonderful adventures to share
from Little Tiger Press

For information regarding any of the above titles or for our catalogue, please contact us:
Little Tiger Press, 1 The Coda Centre, 189 Munster Road, London SW6 6AW
Tel: 020 7385 6333 • Fax: 020 7385 7333 • E-mail: contact@littletiger.co.uk • www.littletiger.co.uk